VINTAGE R🌀SE MYSTERIES

VCR FROM BEYOND

EVAN JACOBS

VINTAGE ROSE MYSTERIES

The Secret Room

Lucky Me

New Painting

Call Waiting

SADDLEBACK
EDUCATIONAL PUBLISHING
www.sdlback.com

ISBN: 978-1-68021-760-5
eBook: 978-1-64598-067-4

Printed in Malaysia

24 23 22 21 20   1 2 3 4 5

THE HISTORY OF THE VINTAGE ROSE ANTIQUE SHOP

The story begins with a sorcerer named Ervin Legend. He had a talent for making money. While traveling, Ervin bought items all over the world. He would have called himself a collector. Others might say hoarder. Once he grew tired of things, he sold them for a profit. "One man's junk is another man's treasure," he used to say.

Eventually, Ervin wanted to settle down. His home was in Scarecrow, California. But he needed somewhere to put all of his things. Ervin opened the Vintage Rose Antique Shop in 1912. It was a place to keep his collections. His wife, Visalia, inspired the shop's name. She loved roses and kept them in vases all over the shop. "Roses mask the smell of old things," she would say.

After the shop opened, Ervin kept traveling. He collected pieces to sell from all over. In 1949, Ervin and Visalia went to Cairo, Egypt. While there, the couple disappeared. Nobody knows what happened to them. Some say Ervin's love of sorcery might have been to blame. He may have looked into something he shouldn't have.

Family members took over the shop. None were quite like Ervin, though. Without his passion, the business began to fail. His sister believed it was cursed.

In 1979, the Legends put the shop up for sale. Rose Myers bought it. She was odd, like Ervin. Her passion for old things was like his. "Everything has a story," she would say, with a twinkle in her eye. From a young age, Rose had looked for bargains. She would resell things for a profit. Buying the Vintage Rose was her dream come true. The place was old. It was filled with odd treasures. Plus, Rose was part of the name of the store. It seemed like this was meant to be.

Rose ran the shop for 40 years. When she passed away, it closed. The business had been left to her nephew, Evan Stewart. He was Rose's closest living relative. The Stewart family moved to Scarecrow. They reopened the shop in 2019.

Today, the shop still holds many treasures. Collectors come from all over. Some have purchased these mysterious relics. Are they magical? Do they watch over the store? We may never find out. Or will we?

CHAPTER 1

REWIND

Achoo!" The sneeze startles me, and I almost knock over a vase. Across the room, Alex is flipping through a book. A cloud of dust rises from the pages.

"Little Alex," Mark sighs. "What are you doing with that old math book? It doesn't have the answers to tomorrow's quiz! Donovan, can you believe this kid?"

I laugh. It's hard not to. Alex, or Little Alex as we call him, is always doing goofy things. He's a year younger than Mark and me. Little Alex started hanging out with us when he moved to our town four years ago. Mark and I have been friends since first grade. We're in seventh grade now, and Alex is in sixth. Sometimes it's fun to give our younger friend a hard time. He knows we don't mean it.

"All the stuff in here," I giggle. "And Little Alex picks up a math book."

The three of us are at the Vintage Rose Antique Shop. It's a small store in Scarecrow, California, where we live. An old lady named Rose used to own it, but she died around a year ago. Her family took over the shop. They didn't change it much though. The place is still full of weird old stuff. Sometimes we come here after school to look around.

Kids spending time in an antique store after school might sound strange. But there's nothing else to do in our town. Scarecrow has got to be the most boring place on earth. It's just houses, strip malls, and a few parks. The sun never comes out. Even in the summer, the sky is gray.

I pick up an old watch. A small cloud of dust swirls when I lift it. There's a watch-shaped outline on the dusty shelf.

Mark sneezes. He's checking out a piggy bank that looks like it came from my grandma's house. Everything is thrown together on shelves and barely organized.

All this old stuff gives me the creeps. Most of the people who owned it are probably dead now. The thought makes me shiver. I quickly put the watch down.

Mark and I walk over to where Alex is, in the pass-along section. This is the coolest thing about the store. You can take something for free. Then you're supposed to donate something. It's meant to be a way for the community to share. We take stuff sometimes. But we've never donated. It doesn't seem like anyone keeps track.

"I thought the book could help me," Alex says. "There's no way I'm going to pass Mr. Harlin's quiz."

Mr. Harlin is a sixth grade math teacher at our school. He's really mean. Mark and I had him last year. We both hated him. I still passed the class though. Mark didn't. Now he's repeating sixth grade math. It isn't because Mark isn't smart enough. He just never did any work. Alex and Mark have Mr. Harlin for the same period this year.

As we move through the store, I notice a strange smell. It reminds me of roses but not good-smelling ones. This smells like roses that have been in a vase for too long. I guess it only makes sense for a store called Vintage Rose to smell like stale old roses.

A high school kid sits behind the shop's counter. He doesn't pay any attention to us. All he does is stare at his phone.

"This is rad!" Alex says. He picks up a small TV. It has a VCR built into it. Alex pushes the VCR door open with his finger. "Look! There's even a tape in it."

"So what?" Mark says.

"It's only ten dollars."

"That's a rip-off," I say.

"Are you thinking of buying that?" the kid behind the counter asks. He pulls out a thick, ratty-looking blue book and opens it.

"Let's see here," he starts. "That thing came from an estate sale. Someone named Dr. Harry Yates owned it. He was a scientist who tried to create hybrids in his lab. One of his ideas was to mix animals and technology."

The kid slams the blue book shut. "All right." He finally looks at us. "I'm done playing salesman. You want that thing or not? It's ten dollars. Take it or leave it. And it doesn't have a remote so don't even ask."

"I'll take it!" Alex walks over to the counter. He sets the TV/VCR on top of it. "This thing is legit retro."

"Don't buy that," Mark says. "It's junk. You don't even know if it works. There's no remote—"

"So bring it back," the kid behind the counter snaps. "If it doesn't work, we'll refund you." He glares at Mark. "Keep talking and I'm going to raise the price on your friend."

Alex reaches into his pocket and pulls out a crumpled ten-dollar bill. "Guys," he says. "My grandpa gave me a bunch of movies on VHS, remember? Now I can finally watch them!"

CHAPTER 2

STOKED MODE

I can't believe you wasted ten dollars, Little Alex," Mark says.

He's still throwing shade on Alex's purchase. I keep my mouth shut. Alex is totally stoked. Mark is right though. That TV/VCR looks ancient.

It's starting to get dark. We walk past some shops. A few of them are closed already. Most places in downtown Scarecrow shut down early.

"Now I can watch that *Star Wars* tape," he says. I've never seen Alex smile so much. "You guys ever see *The Terminator*?"

"You can stream all of that!" Mark says. "Everybody knows VHS tapes are the worst. That's why they made DVDs."

"And those are practically gone now too!" I point to the TV/VCR. "It looks like nobody has used that thing since 1984."

"My DVD player broke," Alex says. "And I don't

have Netflix. My parents said they *might* get me a new phone for Christmas. But they probably can't afford one. It's not like I can watch stuff on my school tablet."

Mark looks at me and snickers.

I feel bad and look away. Alex's family doesn't have a lot of money. They rent a tiny, two-bedroom house. His neighborhood isn't nearly as nice as the one Mark and I live in. All the houses are small and close together. Cars are packed like sardines on the streets and driveways. Some are even on the lawns. Many of the cars are broken down. They sit on blocks and are missing wheels or have big dents in them.

"Look," I say, changing the subject. "Anyone want to go to the school dance?"

We're walking by Scarecrow Middle School. All the windows in the big, white stone building are black. The gym and multipurpose room rise up behind the main building like dark pillars. At night, the place looks sort of like a modern castle. A banner about the fall dance hangs over the building's main doors.

"Heck no!" Mark laughs.

Alex shrugs. "It might be fun."

He's usually not into school events. That's one of the things Mark, Alex, and I have in common. We just don't care much about school. None of us are involved in activities. After class, we like to play video games or look at memes on our phones. At least that's what Mark and I do. Alex has an old hand-me-down phone that only lets him make calls and send texts. It's pretty useless, but at least he can text us with it.

"Uh, I was joking," I say. Maybe Alex's excitement over his new TV/VCR has made him delusional.

"We should probably head home," Mark says, looking at me.

"No way," Alex says. He holds up the TV/VCR. "You guys are going to help me set this up, right?"

❧ CHAPTER 3 ❧

FRIENDS?

You forgot your key?" Mark rolls his eyes.

"It's okay," Alex says, shutting the old screen door. He walks down the steps in front of his house.

Brown paint is peeling off the one-story home. A few black shingles are missing from the roof. Barely any grass grows in the small front yard.

Alex readjusts the TV/VCR in his arms. He walks to the back of the house. Mark and I follow him.

"I hate coming here," Mark says under his breath.

It's not my favorite place to be either. But I don't say anything. This is Alex's house. I don't want to make him feel bad.

We're standing at the back door. Alex looks around. Then he turns the knob and opens the door.

"You guys leave the door unlocked?" I ask. "*Here?*"

"Yeah. It's because I'm always losing my key. My parents got tired of making me new ones. They can't afford it."

"You really need to get it together, Little Alex," Mark says. "If I lived here, I'd never leave the door unlocked."

"Why not?"

Alex walks into his house. Mark looks at me with big eyes. He can't believe Alex doesn't get it. I shake my head and follow them both inside.

Right away, Alex heads to his room. Mark grabs me and pulls me into the kitchen.

"Alex," Mark calls. "You got anything to eat? I'm starving."

Mark opens the refrigerator. It's practically empty. He cracks up.

I look in the pantry. What we're doing is kind of rude, I guess. Alex doesn't seem to mind though. It sounds like he's moving things around in his room. He's so excited about the TV/VCR that he probably doesn't even remember we're here.

Eventually, I find an unopened package of cookies.

"Hey, can we have these coo—"

Before I finish, Mark grabs the package. He rips it open and stuffs a few cookies in his mouth.

I can't help but laugh. Then I take a bunch of cookies too.

CHAPTER 4

BLACK DOT

An hour later, Alex's TV/VCR is finally set up. It took us a lot longer than it should have. All we really had to do was move some stuff and plug it in. But Mark and I were messing around. We started wrestling and knocked over Alex's bookshelf. Books went all over the floor.

Alex's room was already messy. There were clothes and toys everywhere. I don't think it would've mattered if we didn't clean up the books. But Alex said we had to clean them up. Mark and I helped a little. It was hard because we were laughing too much.

Eventually, Alex cleared off a small chair. He set his broken DVD player on it. Then he put the TV/VCR on top. It's right across from his bed.

Now we're all staring at the blank screen. Alex presses the eject button. The TV/VCR makes a low, whirring noise.

"Are you trying to get the tape out?" I ask.

11

"Yeah."

"It sounds like it's dying," Mark says.

Alex presses eject again. The same thing happens.

"Darn it."

"I told you this thing was junk," Mark says. "Come on, Donovan. Let's bail."

Mark walks out of Alex's room.

Alex starts pressing other buttons. Suddenly, the TV screen is blue. It says *PLAY* in white letters at the top.

Then it goes to a white screen. There's a big black dot in the middle of it.

Mark comes back in. He looks at the TV. Then he looks at me. We burst out laughing.

"Dude!" Mark says. He's laughing so hard he can barely talk. "You just blew ten bucks!"

"Whatever," Alex says.

He sits on the bed and stares at the TV screen. His eyes are glued to the black dot. It almost looks like he's in a trance.

"You're not really into this," I say to him. "Are you?"

I figure Alex is clowning us. He doesn't want to admit he wasted his money.

"It's interesting," Alex says quietly.

He's concentrating completely on the screen. I look at it again. All I see is a boring black dot.

Mark grabs me and drags me out of the room.

"Bye, Little Alex," I call.

Alex, who always says goodbye, doesn't say anything.

The two of us go out the back door.

CHAPTER 5

MIKE AND IKE

It's really dark out now. The wind has picked up. There's a chill in the air.

Mark and I walk faster. All we have on are our Thrasher windbreakers. Even though we don't skateboard, we like to wear the clothes. Neither of us ever wears a heavy jacket.

"I haven't even looked at my math homework since school started," Mark says.

"Really?"

I try to keep up on my schoolwork as much as I can. It's not because it interests me. Passing my classes just makes life easier. The last thing I need are my parents and teachers harassing me about my grades.

"Mark," I say. "You don't want be an eighth grader taking sixth grade math."

"What does it matter?" he says, laughing. "They'll push me through no matter what."

"Yeah, but you'll have Mr. Harlin for *three* years. Nobody wants that!"

I can tell Mark is thinking about this. He looks at the ground as we walk. "Maybe you're right."

"Math with Mrs. Chow is way better," I say, smiling. "You know Grace and Kimberly are in my class."

"Don't rub it in, bro."

Grace and Kimberly are two girls we've known since elementary school. Everyone likes them. Both play on the girls' soccer team. They're in all kinds of clubs too. Unlike us, they care about school. Everything seems easy for them.

Mark has a crush on Grace. She always looks so serious. Maybe it's her dark hair and glasses. I have a crush on Kimberly, who is always laughing. They are the perfect complement to each other. Both of us are shy around them. But Alex won't even look at them, much less talk to them.

"You should ask Grace to the school dance!" I grin.

"Are you crazy?" Mark pushes me. "She'd *never* go to the dance with me."

"You never know!" I crack up. Grace and Kimberly barely know Mark and I are alive. They wouldn't know what to do if one of us asked them to the dance.

"Grace is in my English class," Mark says. "We talk sometimes. She doesn't seem to hate me."

"Then you're in! Just ask her. What's the worst thing she can say?"

"Uh . . . no?"

Now Mark is laughing too.

"Big deal. If she says no, you can ask her again next year."

"I'm not asking her out every year!" Mark snaps. He's laughing harder now. "That's way creepy."

"It's better than doing nothing."

"You ask Kimberly," Mark says. "Then maybe I'll ask Grace."

"No way!"

"Why not? What's the worst thing she can say?" Now it's Mark's turn to laugh at me.

Suddenly, something whizzes past my head. I duck. Mark does too. Was that a rock? We both look in the direction it came from. It's too dark to see who threw it.

"Sorry," a voice says. "I was aiming for your friend!" Then two people start laughing like maniacs.

Mark looks at me with wide eyes. "Is that who I think it is?"

At that moment, the owners of the voices step out

from behind a big tree. It's Mike and Isaac. They are high schoolers who always mess with everybody. Both of them are tall and thick. Their oversized hoodies make them look even bigger. Mike is holding some rocks.

Before we can run, they're hovering over us. Their faces are inches from ours. The bullies are so close, I can smell their bad breath. I'm guessing they ate pizza for dinner.

A chill runs through my whole body. How will we get out of this?

CHAPTER 6

NARROW ESCAPE

Were these geeks talking about girls?" Mike says.

"It sounded like they were," Isaac laughs.

Then their laughter turns to cackling.

Nobody likes these guys. Most of the kids in our middle school fear them. Everybody calls them Mike and Ike, like the candy. But it's a bad idea to call them that to their faces. They have been known to fight people over it.

"Look," Mark says. "Donovan and I are just walking home. We don't want any trouble."

"That's too bad," Mike says. "Because you dweebs found it!" He lifts up his big hands and pushes both of us.

The force of the push makes us fly back five feet. These guys are looking for a fight. They don't care that we don't want one. It doesn't matter that we're younger and smaller.

Mark and I clench our fists. Fear fills my body. I've

never been in a real fight. This seems crazy. We were just walking home. How did we get into this mess?

Mike and Isaac are coming toward us. I close my eyes.

"You boys leave them alone!" a voice calls.

We all turn around and look. An old lady is standing on her porch. She leans against a walker and holds up her flip phone.

"I'm calling the police!"

The bullies look startled.

"Later," Mark smiles.

"Yeah, see you, Mike and Ike!"

I laugh at my own joke. Mark does too as we take off running.

Mike and Isaac don't follow us. We chuckle all the way home. That situation was so intense, it made me forget how cold I am.

A few hours later, most of my homework is done. It's never all finished. There's too much. I do what I can, and my teachers are usually okay with that. They have so many students. It's not like they have time to worry a lot about me.

I lie on my bed and look around. There's a big TV in my room. Video games and a few books sit on a shelf next to it. Clothes hang neatly in the closet. My parents make me keep my room clean. If they didn't care, it would probably be messy like Alex's. But I would still have nice stuff. Little Alex was so excited about that old TV/VCR. I guess I'm pretty lucky.

Before bed, I decide to play a game. Mark and I love to play *Clan Castles* online together. The goal is to defeat the kings in as many castles as possible. I check to see if he's on right now. His avatar doesn't show up, so I text him.

Donovan

get on

That's all I need to say. Mark will know exactly what I'm talking about.

Mark

Donovan

eating, b on later

k

Then I look through my messages. Alex hasn't texted me all night. Mark and I messaged him earlier. We told him how Mike and Ike messed with us. Little Alex always texts us back. Maybe his old phone finally died. It's also possible he's too busy watching VHS tapes on his new TV/VCR. The thought makes me laugh.

CHAPTER 7

ODD BEHAVIOR

Did you beat that king?" I ask Mark the next morning. Both of us stayed up too late playing *Clan Castles*. Now we're at school. The first period bell is going to ring any minute.

"Yeah," he says, laughing. "I can't believe you got taken out by a sentry."

"He came out of nowhere!"

The halls are packed with students. Most are staring at their phones or their school tablets. Signs for the upcoming fall dance are on every wall.

"Hey, there's Grace and Kimberly," I say, pointing.

The friends glide down the hall toward us. It's almost as if the other kids part to let them through. Grace is wearing a black hoodie. "Girl Power" is written on it in pink letters.

"Say something to them," I whisper to Mark. "Talk to Grace about the English homework. Then ask her to the dance."

Mark looks at me and grins. "Okay."

"Really?"

Did he only say that so I'd be quiet?

Grace and Kimberly are about to walk by. Mark stares at Grace. I'm not sure he even knows I'm still here. Maybe he really is going to ask her out.

"Hey, Grace," Mark says, smiling. "You finish the English assignment?"

"Yeah," Grace says. "Did *you?*" She laughs.

"Sort of," Mark says.

The girls continue walking. They're not going to stop just to talk to us.

"Hey, want to go to the fall dance with me?" Mark says.

I can't believe it. He actually asked her. There's no smile on his face either. Maybe he wants to make sure Grace doesn't think it's a joke.

Everyone around us stops. Kids look up from their electronics. It's silent. We all wait for Grace's answer.

"Um," Grace says. She looks away. "I . . . already have a date. But why don't you ask Kimberly?"

"Ew," Kimberly says. There's a grimace on her face. "No way!"

The two girls laugh and walk away. Everyone around us goes back to looking at their phones and tablets.

Mark stares after them even as we start walking again. I put my arm around him.

"Whatever," I say. "There are other girls."

"Who cares," Mark says. "It's not like I'm going to that dumb dance anyway."

"Exactly."

Across the hallway, we see Little Alex. He's watching something on his school tablet. Alex holds the screen close to his face.

As we get closer, I see Alex's lips moving. He's smiling a lot too.

"Is he video chatting with someone?" Mark asks.

I was wondering the same thing. Sometimes Mark says exactly what I'm thinking. It's like our brains are connected.

"He wouldn't do that in school. Especially not on his school tablet. Right?"

"Besides," Mark says. "We're his only friends. Who would he be chatting with?"

"He's probably watching *SpongeBob*."

We crack up. Alex still loves to watch cartoons. Mark and I give him a hard time about it. Our favorite show is *Stranger Things*. Little Alex says it's too scary.

As we get closer, Alex spots us. The smile leaves

his face. His eyebrows narrow. Our friend almost seems to be scowling at us. I've never seen him look at anyone like this before.

"What are you watching, Little Alex?" I ask.

He quickly shuts off his tablet.

"Nothing," he snaps.

CHAPTER 8

LITTLE ALEX NO MORE

Alex clutches his tablet to his chest. It feels like we interrupted something important.

"What's up?" Mark asks. "We saw you talking to your tablet. Were you video chatting?"

"No!"

He continues to stare at us. I've never seen Alex this standoffish.

"Look," I say. "Sorry we messed around at your house yesterday. How's the new TV/VCR working?"

I grin and Mark starts laughing. Maybe this will lighten the mood.

It doesn't work on Alex. "The TV is awesome," he yells. "Just like I thought it would be. And no, I wasn't video chatting."

Alex holds up his tablet now. He starts talking even louder.

"You two losers wouldn't understand what I'm

doing. And stop calling me Little Alex. It's just *Alex*. Got it?" His face turns to a scowl again.

The bell rings.

"Got it," Mark mumbles. Neither of us smiles.

Alex turns and walks away. All the students head to first period.

Later, Mark and I walk home from school together. We talk about how weird Alex was this morning.

"I didn't see him all day," Mark says. "Except in math. He wasn't paying attention at all. Normally, he asks a bunch of questions. Today he just stared at his tablet, holding it really close to his face. Mr. Harlin didn't seem to notice."

"This feels strange," I say. "Usually Alex walks with us."

"Yeah," Mark agrees. "I don't know what's going on with him."

"What should we do today? I want some candy."

"Okay. Let's go to Reggie's."

Scarecrow Plaza is one of the biggest strip malls in town. There are a bunch of stores there. One is an old-fashioned candy shop called Reggie's. It also has ice cream cones, shakes, and malts. We like to go there after school sometimes.

On our way to Reggie's, Mark and I take out our

phones. We check our messages. Then Mark shares a funny video with me. We are laughing at it when a rock flies at us. It bounces off my shoulder.

"Ouch!" I yelp.

Before turning around, I already know who threw it. Mike and Ike walk out from behind a brick wall. It runs next to some apartments.

"Bull's-eye!" Mike says. He takes aim with another rock.

"Are you guys ready to finish what we started?" Isaac asks.

It's not really a question. These bullies don't care about our answer. We are in big trouble. I don't think anybody is going to save us today.

Mark and I turn to run. But two more kids come at us from the other direction. We know these guys. They're Mike and Ike's brothers. Rusty looks just like Mike. James is a short version of Isaac. Both of them are eighth graders at Scarecrow Middle School. As their brothers close in on us, they laugh.

"Four against two? Come on!" Mark cries. "This isn't fair."

Mike grabs him. He gets Mark in a headlock.

Isaac reaches for me. I swat his hand away.

"You called us Mike and Ike. Everyone knows

how we feel about that." Mike tightens his hold on Mark's neck.

"Sorry," Mark gasps.

"Too late!" Isaac comes toward me now. He winds up to throw a punch. I dive off to the side. The punch misses me by inches.

Mike still has a hold on Mark. I can hear my friend choking.

As I scramble to get up, Rusty and James come toward me.

"Where do you think you're going?" Rusty says. I'm on my hands and knees. James puts his foot on my back. Isaac looms over me.

This is it. There's no escaping now. I close my eyes and brace for the attack.

"What the—" Isaac yells suddenly.

"Look out!" Rusty shouts.

James takes his foot off my back. I open my eyes to see what's going on.

Someone is spinning around like a tornado. His arms are outstretched. I watch as he hits Isaac. The bully goes flying at least 15 feet.

Rusty and James are running away. They don't even look back to see if their brothers are okay.

Now the human tornado heads straight for Mike.

Mark slips out of the headlock. He runs in the other direction. Mike just stands there with wide eyes. The tornado makes contact and hurls him even farther than Isaac.

The bullies are rolling on the ground, moaning. I get on my feet. Mark and I look around. What just happened?

CHAPTER 9

TEARFUL HERO

Who is that?" I whisper.

The tornado slows down. It starts to look like a person.

Mark's jaw drops. "You?" he says.

It's Alex. Neither of us can believe it.

Mike and Isaac stagger to their feet. Alex takes one step toward them. They both put their arms up in surrender. Then the bullies run away.

"Dude!" Mark says. "Little Alex! Um, I mean Alex . . . how . . . what . . .?"

Alex stares at us. It's almost like he doesn't recognize Mark and me. His breathing is heavy.

"That was lit!" I say. "Where did you learn that?"

Alex breathes heavier. He seems to be panting. His mouth opens wider and wider.

All of a sudden, he bursts into tears. Our friend starts bawling right in front of us. He used to cry a lot in elementary school. Sometimes it was for no reason. If a teacher called his name, Alex would assume he was in trouble. But we haven't seen him cry in a while.

"Alex," Mark says. "It's cool. You didn't do anything wrong."

"Yeah," I say. "They were messing with us. You saved us. They got what they deserved."

Alex is crying even harder now. Mark takes a step toward him.

Without warning, Alex runs away. He's fast. The kid has never run like this in P.E. It doesn't even look like him as he goes.

Mark and I take off after him. There's no way we can keep up. His speed is superhuman. Eventually, we both stop running.

"Wow," Mark says, gasping for air. "That was insane. I'd never in a million years think Alex could do something like that."

"We didn't even know it was him." I'm breathing heavily too. Mark and I should start trying harder in P.E. "Why did he run away? It was like that wasn't really him or something."

"He's been acting weird. Maybe he just doesn't want to talk to anyone right now?"

"Maybe. Or he's tired? Becoming a human tornado probably takes a lot out of you."

CHAPTER 10

LADIES' MAN

I check my phone. After the fight yesterday, we texted Alex to make sure he was okay. Since then, I've been checking my phone every chance I get. Neither of us has gotten a response yet.

At first, we figured he was still mad at us. He got so worked up when we teased him about his TV/VCR.

It's true that Mark and I treat Alex like a little kid sometimes. We never ask him what *he* wants to do. Usually we just tell him what *we're* going to do. The two of us assume Alex will follow along.

That's going to change, I tell myself. When Alex starts talking to us again, it will be different. We're not going to give him such a hard time. Mark and I will treat him like an equal.

At lunch, I sit down next to Mark. The lunchroom is packed with students. The smell of hamburgers fills the room. Every Thursday, they grill hamburgers outside. This is Mark's favorite school lunch. But today he has barely touchcd his burger.

Mark has his school tablet out. He's swiping around on YouTube. At school, YouTube is awful. The cool channels are blocked. All we can watch are educational videos. We're only supposed to use our tablets to help with our schoolwork.

"What's up?" I ask while taking my lunch out of my backpack.

"Nothing." Mark doesn't look up from his tablet.

"All right," I say. "I can deal with Little Alex—I mean Alex—acting weird. But you? No way. You're not even eating your hamburger. What's wrong?"

"Progress reports," Mark says. His tone is lifeless. He still doesn't look up from the tablet.

"Oh." I forgot about those. They were emailed to parents yesterday. Mine was okay. It wasn't great, but I'm passing all my classes.

Mark finally looks at me. "My parents were really upset. They even took away my phone."

That explains why he's using his school tablet.

"I wonder how Alex did?"

"That's another thing," Mark said. "A bunch of kids in Mr. Harlin's class are doing really bad. He yelled at us for the whole period."

"Ugh."

"Then, while he was shouting at us, Alex *yawned*."

"No way!" Mr. Harlin hates when students are tired. He says there are 24 hours in a day. We have time to get all the sleep we need.

"Mr. Harlin started yelling at him. It was crazy."

"What did Alex do? He didn't start crying, did he?"

"Nope. Alex just stared at Mr. Harlin. He didn't say a word. That made Mr. Harlin even madder. I was kind of impressed, actually."

"Wow. I wonder what's going on with him."

Mark shrugs and goes back to his tablet.

I'm about to take a bite out of my peanut butter and jelly sandwich. It has a lot of jelly in it. My dad knows that's how I like it.

Then I see Alex. He comes into the lunchroom. But our friend is not alone.

"Is that Alex walking with . . . Grace and Kimberly?" Mark asks.

Almost everybody in the lunchroom gets quiet. We all stare. Alex talks to Grace and Kimberly. They actually talk back to him. The girls seem to laugh at everything he says. After getting their hamburgers, the three walk out.

Kimberly and Grace never eat in the lunchroom.

They walk around school during lunch. Now apparently Alex is going with them.

"After yesterday, I thought I'd seen everything," Mark says. "First, Alex becomes a human tornado. He sends two high school bullies running. Now he's hanging out with Grace and Kimberly? This is totally bananas."

I shake my head in disbelief. "It's more like Grace and Kimberly are hanging out with *him*."

CHAPTER 11

TOO COOL FOR SCHOOL

Alex!" Mark calls.

He doesn't turn around. School just let out. We try to catch Alex to walk home with us, but he's moving too fast. His school tablet is right in front of his face again.

"What's he doing?" I ask. "The school Wi-Fi doesn't even extend this far."

"Who cares," Mark says. He starts to jog. "We need to find out about Grace and Kimberly."

I start jogging too. For a moment, Mark and I have to break into a full run. That's how fast Alex is walking.

"Alex," I shout when we get close to him. "Slow down."

"We're your friends, remember?" Mark calls.

Again, Alex quickly puts his tablet down. He shuts it off.

"What are you watch . . ." I start to ask. Then I trail off. It's clear Alex doesn't want to answer.

"Sup?" Alex asks. He looks straight ahead. It's like he doesn't even see Mark and me.

Alex has never said things like "Sup?" before. He was always happy to talk to us. What happened to our friend?

"Bro," Mark says. "What's up with Grace and Kimberly?"

"What do you mean?" Alex asks, smirking.

"Alex," I say. "You were scared to even talk to them before. Now you're hanging out with them at lunch?"

"Do they both like you?" Mark asks.

"I don't know," he says. For a moment, he seems to be thinking. I wonder if perhaps the old Alex might still be here. Then he says, "I haven't decided how much *I* like *them*."

Mark and I look at each other. This is bizarre. Alex has never gotten much attention from girls. Now he's being picky about them? It's like he's a different person.

"What do you mean?" Mark asks.

"Grace and Kimberly both like me. They keep bugging me about the dance."

"About who you're going to take?"

"I'm taking both of them," Alex says. His smirk is even bigger now. "They're fighting over who will get to dance with me first. See you guys later."

Alex turns down another street. He's moving fast again.

"Bye," I call after him.

"Are you going to study for Mr. Harlin's quiz?" Mark yells.

"Never," Alex shouts. "I hate that guy."

He lifts his tablet to his face again. Something white comes on the screen. That's all I can see.

None of this is normal for Alex. He used to try so hard in Mr. Harlin's class. It wasn't just math either. In all his classes, he did his best. Alex hated getting in trouble with teachers.

"You think Alex is still doing work in his other classes?" I ask Mark.

"Who knows? Maybe he just hates Mr. Harlin. I do too. But I'm going to start doing my homework more."

I can't believe my ears. First Alex starts acting weird, and now Mark too?

"What?" he asks. Mark can tell I'm surprised. "Christmas is less than four weeks away. If my grades are still bad, my parents aren't going to be happy. If they're not happy, they won't get me anything good. I'm not going to mess with that!"

Okay, so Mark is still the same. But something is up with Alex.

CHAPTER 12

MORNING SURPRISE

Donovan

it's freezing ❄️

Mark

mom is driving me

Donovan

cool. c u there.

I walk to school in the freezing cold alone. There's a hoodie under my windbreaker, but I'm still cold. Maybe I should start wearing a real coat.

Even though it's cold, I don't mind the walk. Having some alone time is good. It gives me a chance to think.

Mostly, my mind is on Alex. What is going on with him? I try to think back to when this all started. Mark and I were rude at his house that one day. We're always like that though. Alex never seemed to mind before.

Did something change that day? We did diss his new purchase. Alex bought that silly TV/VCR from the weird Vintage Rose. He was so stoked that he was going to be able to watch VHS tapes in his room.

Thinking about it still makes me laugh. Why would he care so much about that?

I'm turning the corner now. Scarecrow Middle School is just down the street. There are more people than usual standing out front. In the middle of the crowd, there's a big, red fire truck. An ambulance is there too. Its lights are flashing. Everybody has their phones out.

"What's going on?" I whisper to myself. Then I start to slowly jog toward school.

Soon I'm close enough to see paramedics bringing over a stretcher. An oxygen mask covers the face of the person on it.

Is that . . . Mr. Harlin?

They load him in the ambulance and quickly drive off.

I walk into the crowd of teachers and students in front of the school.

"Mr. Harlin had a heart attack," one of the teachers says.

"They said he just collapsed," another teacher adds. "He might have hit his head too. It could have caused a concussion."

The fire truck leaves, but most people stay outside. Teachers frown and whisper to each other. Students share videos they took of the scene. I run into Nate, a kid who lives in my neighborhood. He's an eighth grader. Nate fills me in on what he has heard.

People said Mr. Harlin came to school early, as usual. He was getting his classroom set up. Then another math teacher, Mrs. Lopez, heard him scream. She said it sounded like he was being murdered.

Mrs. Lopez ran toward the scream. There was a loud thud. When she went into Mr. Harlin's classroom, he was on the floor. She quickly called 911 and campus security.

Mark walks up to me and Nate. He's wearing an oversized black hoodie.

"Wow," I say. "You must be really cold. That's the biggest hoodie I've ever seen."

"Dude, what happened?"

Nate and I tell Mark about Mr. Harlin. Then Nate goes to talk to some other friends.

"Well," Mark laughs. "Maybe we won't have a quiz today."

"Mark!" I say. "That's so not cool. Mr. Harlin isn't the nicest guy in the world. He doesn't deserve a heart attack though."

"You're right." Mark looks down. "It was too soon. Alex will probably be stoked, though."

"The way he's acting, I don't think he cares about anything."

Then I see Alex standing near the front of the school. He's wiping his eyes. It looks like he's . . . crying?

"Or maybe he actually *does* care."

"What are you talking about?" Mark asks. I point at Alex, and Mark looks over. "Is he crying?"

"He did the same thing after saving us from Mike and Ike," I say slowly.

"Yeah. Why?"

I shrug.

Mark's eyes narrow. "You don't think he's really crying over Mr. Harlin, do you?"

"I don't know."

"Let's go ask him," Mark says.

"He's not talking to us, remember?"

"Who cares?"

Mark starts walking toward Alex. I have a feeling this won't go well. Alex used to get scared when people confronted him. But lately he just seems to get mad. We haven't been able to talk to him at all. Still, I follow Mark. Maybe we can get through to our friend.

The bell for first period rings.

"Oh well," I say. "Time to go to class." Secretly, I'm relieved.

We watch as Grace and Kimberly walk up to Alex. He tries to hide his tears.

"I wonder what they'll think of him now," Mark says. "Since he's crying all over the place."

Grace and Kimberly both hug Alex. The three of them walk away. The girls continue to pat Alex on the back.

"Wow!" Mark says. "Little Alex is totally milking it."

"I'm not so sure."

"So what is it? First he takes on Mike and Isaac. Then he starts hanging out with Grace and Kimberly. He totally ditches us. Now he's crying over Mr. Harlin?"

"Let's go to his house after school," I say. "Maybe he'll talk to us there."

CHAPTER 13

THE CREATURE

Alex isn't home," his mom says.

She's talking to us through the screen door. I think we interrupted her while she was getting ready for work. Alex's mom has a second job at a store that sells baby clothes and gear. His dad works a second job too. That's why Alex is home by himself so much.

"Where is he?" I ask.

"I don't know. Look, it's time for me to go to work. I'll let Alex know you stopped by." His mom abruptly shuts the door. We start to walk away.

"That was strange," Mark says.

"Yeah. Even his mom is acting weird."

"She's never like that with us," Mark says.

"Usually she asks us to come in and wait," I say. "She even offers us food. So what should we do now?"

"Wait a second. I have an idea." Mark pulls out his phone and starts swiping around on it. "We can use the Find My Friends app to see where Alex is."

"Alex doesn't have that on his old phone, genius."

"I know," Mark says. "But it's set up on his school tablet."

"Oh!" I say. "Maybe you *are* a genius!"

Mark laughs as I look over at his phone screen. There's a map on it. He taps Alex's name in the list below the map. A blinking dot shows up.

"There he is!" I say.

Mark zooms in on the map. The blinking dot is coming from Alex's house. "And he's home."

I look at Mark. "Let's go back," he says. "We'll knock on his bedroom window."

"What if he gets mad?" I ask.

"Oh well."

We return to Alex's house. This time, we go around to the back. Mark and I peek into his bedroom window.

The room is dark. Only the light from the TV screen illuminates it. Alex is standing next to his bed. He's staring at the big black dot again. His eyes are glued to the screen, just like before.

"Alex!" Mark calls. He raises his hand to knock on the window. I stop him.

"Shh. Let's see what he's doing."

"He's staring at a black dot. What more do we need to see?"

Suddenly, Alex clenches his fists. His mouth opens wide. Tears stream down the sides of his face. He's crying again.

I can hardly believe what happens next.

A slimy black creature crawls out of our friend's mouth. It has big, round, bright green eyes.

The skinny creature jumps to the floor. Slime drips from its body.

How was this thing inside Alex? It must be over two feet tall!

Alex falls onto his bed. Then the creature hops through the black dot into the TV. In seconds, it's gone.

"What in the world did we just see?" Mark asks.

My heart races. Is our friend okay? Did that creature just kill him?

"Alex!" I yell. "Alex!"

Mark yells too. But Alex doesn't move.

CHAPTER 14

DR. YATES

Mark and I run back around to the front of the house. We pound on the door. Alex's mom opens it. She looks really annoyed now.

"Um, hi again," Mark says, smiling. "We were just wondering if Alex was home yet?"

"Boys, I told you he's not here. You're going to make me late for work."

"Can you please just check?" I beg. "Maybe he's being really quiet in his room?"

Alex's mom sighs. But she doesn't shut the door. She walks down the hall. We hear her open his bedroom door. Mark and I hold our breath.

A minute later, she comes back. "Sorry, boys. He's asleep. If he wakes up soon, I'll tell him you stopped by."

"Okay. Thanks," I say. At least we know our friend isn't dead. Mark and I turn around and walk away.

"All right," Mark says. "What are we going to do, Donovan? There's an alien inside our friend!"

"I know." My brain is still trying to process all this. "How in the world does that thing live inside Alex?"

"And how does it disappear into a dot in an old TV?"

I go over the day in my head. "Hey. Do you think Alex showed that creature to Mr. Harlin this morning?" The realization makes my body start to shake.

"You think?"

"Yesterday you said Mr. Harlin yelled at him. Alex didn't even care, right? He probably figured he'd get him later . . . with that creature!"

"Whoa," Mark says. "Maybe Mr. Harlin got so scared, he had a heart attack. Then he fell and hit his head."

"That's all Alex had to do. Then that thing probably crawled back inside him."

"When we saw him this morning, he was crying. Remember?"

"It was the same way he cried after saving us from Mike and Ike," I say.

Every weird thing Alex has done lately is starting to make sense.

"That's why he's been crying," I go on. "The creature must take everything out of him. Alex can't help it. He's crying from exhaustion."

Mark nods. "This all started when Alex got that TV/VCR."

"Yeah," I say. "Didn't the guy at the antique store say the original owner was a scientist?"

"Yeah, Dr. Yates or something."

"Dude, how did you remember that? You really should try harder in school."

"The guy at Vintage Rose said Dr. Yates did weird experiments. He sounded like a mad scientist," Mark says. "I thought that was kind of cool, so I looked him up. There were a bunch of links, but I got distracted before I read much."

I pull out my phone and search for "Dr. Yates weird experiments."

Mark looks over my shoulder as we scan the results. A few articles are from scientific journals. There are also news stories. Some are from the local Scarecrow paper. We skim a few.

"This guy got in big trouble because of his experiments," Mark says.

"Yeah, he was breaking the law. Dr. Yates did

experiments with animals and technology. He tried to merge the two and create hybrids." I scroll through more articles.

"He did experiments with animals and cars . . ."

"Animals and refrigerators . . ."

"Animals and *TVs!*"

Mark and I look at each other in disbelief. We'd both be cracking up if this situation wasn't so serious.

I tap another search result. "This guy was messing with the animals' DNA. That's not cool! He probably created that creature that lives in Alex's TV/VCR."

"And now in Alex."

Mark and I are quiet. We're both too scared to talk.

I continue to read. "His benefactors found out and pulled his funding. A guy named Norman Legend was his biggest benefactor."

"You think he's related to Principal Legend?" Mark asks. That's our principal at Scarecrow Middle School. He's tall with a bushy mustache and huge hands.

"Who knows?" I say. "But it sounds like everyone shunned Dr. Yates when they found out what he was doing."

"Can we find Dr. Yates? Maybe he has changed. He might help us."

"He lost his job teaching at Scarecrow College," I

read from my phone. "Norman Legend personally had him fired. He was furious that his money had been used for those experiments. Dr. Yates vanished after that."

"He's gone? So what are we going to do?"

"Well, the first step is to make Alex get rid of that TV/VCR."

The next day at lunch, Mark and I look for Alex.

"I saw him in Mr. Harlin's class," Mark says. "He must be around here somewhere."

Right then, I see Alex on the field. He's holding his tablet close to his face again. Mark and I rush over.

"Alex," I say. "We know what's going on."

"What?" he snaps.

Alex quickly puts the tablet down. The screen goes black. Mark and I can't see what's on it.

"Hey, Alex!" a voice calls.

All three of us turn around. It's Rusty and James, Mike and Isaac's brothers.

"What you did to our brothers the other day was a cheap shot," Rusty says.

"You won't get away with it," James shouts. "Nobody messes with Mike and Isaac and lives to tell about it!"

CHAPTER 15

THE BEAST OF SCARECROW MIDDLE SCHOOL

Alex starts to cry again.

Mark shoots me a look. We know what that means. The creature is either coming in or going out of Alex. That's why he ran away after scaring off Mike and Ike. He didn't want us to see that creature.

"Crying isn't going to help," Rusty says. He and James laugh. "You didn't cry about hurting our brothers."

"Well," Mark says. "Actually, he did."

"Be quiet!" James yells. "You want us to pound you too?"

Alex is crying harder now. His mouth opens wide.

"Oh no," I say.

Mark grabs me. Before we can run, the slimy creature bursts out of Alex's mouth. It lands right in front of Rusty and James.

"Rooooooaaaar!" the beast howls.

The bullies look like their eyes are going to pop out of their heads. Both of them start screaming. They take off toward the blacktop.

The creature breathes heavily. Its body heaves up and down. Slime drips off its head and onto the grass.

Alex continues to cry. Tears pour down his cheeks. He doesn't even try to hide them.

"Alex," I say, putting my hand on his shoulder. "It's—"

Before I can finish saying "It's okay," the creature grabs him. Then it takes off across the field, dragging Alex like a rag doll. The beast jumps over the school fence. It still has Alex. Within a couple of minutes, they are out of sight.

"Whoa!" Mark says. "Did that just happen?"

"I think so."

"He's over here!" we hear Rusty yell.

James and Rusty are running across the field toward us. Principal Legend is with them. So is Mr. Williamson, the campus security guard. Mr. Williamson always wears track suits and a green hat. He's tall and muscular.

"Where'd he go?" James asks. "He was right here!"

"Yeah," Rusty says. "Then that thing came out of his mouth!"

Mark and I stare at them.

"What are you talking about?" I ask innocently.

"Liar! You know. Your friend . . . he . . . he threw up that *thing!*"

"What?" I laugh. Mark does too.

"Where's Alex?" Principal Legend asks.

"He's not here," I say quickly.

"Yeah," Mark says. "He came to school, but then he went home sick."

It's kind of true. Alex was here. He just left without permission.

"These guys are always messing with people," I say. "You know their brothers, Mike and Ike? They're the same way."

"So Alex went home sick?" Mr. Williamson asks.

"Yeah," I say. "I'm not sure what period. He was here this morning."

"Okay," Principal Legend says. "Rusty, James, come with us."

"But we didn't do anything!" Rusty protests. "They're totally lying for their friend!"

"Let's go," Mr. Williamson says in a stern voice.

"Why are *we* in trouble?" James asks.

Mr. Williamson ushers them away. Rusty and James keep looking back. They shake their heads and raise their fists at Mark and me.

"I guess they're after us now too," Mark says. "It's kind of cool having two whole families after you."

"Who cares," I say.

"You know it's only a matter of time before Principal Legend figures out that Alex left without permission," Mark says. "They'll probably think he ditched and that we covered for him."

"We just need to get through sixth period," I say. Thankfully, that's right after lunch. "Then we'll go back to Alex's house."

CHAPTER 16

HISTORY REPORT

Mark and I sit in Principal Legend's office. He called us here during sixth period. I'm staring at my feet and trying to act cool. Inside, my heart is pounding.

"Donovan, Mark, I need your help with something," the principal says. "Earlier you said your friend Alex had gone home sick today. Our records show that Alex reported to classes this morning. But he was never sent to the office for illness."

Principal Legend pauses. I think he expects us to explain. Mark and I keep our mouths shut.

He goes on. "Alex didn't show up for sixth period. Do you know where he might be?"

Mark looks over at me. Then he looks at Principal Legend.

"Sir, the last time I saw Alex was in math. We both have Mr. Harlin third period. He told me his stomach hurt."

I follow Mark's lead. "Yeah, and then he wasn't at lunch. So we just figured . . ."

"He must have gone home sick." Mark shrugs.

The principal stares at us without saying anything. I feel my face get hot. Maybe he senses we're lying. But how do we explain that our friend has been taken over by a slimy alien creature that came out of an old TV/VCR?

Then I get an idea.

"Principal Legend, I'm glad you called us in."

His eyes narrow. "You are?"

"Yeah. See, we're working on a report for history class. It's about Scarecrow. In our research, we read about a guy named Norman Legend. Is there any chance you're related?"

Surprise flashes across Principal Legend's face.

"Norman Legend, you say?"

"Yep. Do you know him?"

"Actually, yes." He touches his mustache. "Norman was my uncle. He was a dean at Scarecrow College. Science was his passion."

"Oh, cool!" Mark jumps in. "So, uh . . . did he ever do anything interesting? You know, like weird experiments?"

I cough. "We found an article online. It talked

about Dr. Harry Yates. Sounds like he did some pretty crazy stuff!"

Principal Legend frowns. Then he gives us a serious look. "Boys, my uncle's life was disrupted by scandal. Harry Yates was the source of it. He was not a good man. But Uncle Norm put a stop to everything. As soon as he found out, he had Dr. Yates fired. My uncle never wanted anybody to get hurt."

Mark and I nod. Maybe Norman Legend can help us after all. We just have to get Principal Legend to help us find him.

"Wow, sir," I say. "Does your uncle live nearby? Could we talk to him? For our report, I mean."

"I'm afraid not," he says. "After the scandal, Uncle Norm became reclusive. He rarely left his house. All he did was watch movies on a small TV. My aunt would find him mumbling to himself. Something about wicked creatures in evil TVs. Sometimes he just stared at the blank screen. She took him to doctors. They put him in a rest home. About five years ago, he passed away."

Mark and I look at each other. "Oh no," I say. "I'm so sorry."

"They said it was from stress. The scandal really upset him. Aunt Sally got rid of everything related to the experiments. I think she sold a bunch of things to the Vintage Rose shop. You know, my grandfather Ervin Legend once owned that place. Anyway, Uncle Norm used to tell us to burn everything. He said that was the only way to get rid of the bad energy. But Sally was just happy to get it out of the house."

We're quiet. Principal Legend seems bummed out now.

"Anyway, are you sure you don't know where your friend Alex is?"

Mark and I shake our heads.

"Okay. If you see him, please tell him to come to my office first thing tomorrow. You can go now. Oh, and good luck with your history report."

CHAPTER 17

GRAND THEFT TV/VCR

After school, Mark and I head straight to Alex's house. We have to get that TV/VCR. If we don't, our friend might end up like Norman Legend.

When we get there, no cars are in the driveway. We knock on the door. Nobody answers.

"Maybe he's in his room?" I say.

We walk around to the back of the house and peek through his window.

"What if he sees us?" Mark asks. "And gets really mad? I don't want that thing coming after me."

"Me neither."

Alex isn't in his room.

"What if we just sneak in and take the TV/VCR?" Mark says.

"You mean, like, steal it?"

"Well, we know it's dangerous. Principal Legend said all the stuff from the experiments was cursed! We've got to do something."

"What if that thing is still in Alex?" I ask. "If we take the TV, will it be stuck inside him forever?"

"I think it's worth the risk," Mark says. "Come on. Alex or his mom could come home any minute."

"But—"

Before I can finish, Mark opens the back door.

"It's always open, remember?" he says. "Because Alex forgets his key so much."

"This is a bad idea," I say. Still, I follow him into the house.

Mark and I tiptoe into Alex's room. Oddly, it's neat and tidy now. His clothes and toys aren't all over the place.

"Maybe that creature cleans up too," Mark says, laughing.

We both eye the TV/VCR. It just sits there. Nothing about it seems scary or dangerous.

"You don't think the creature could be here, do you?" I ask. "Like outside the TV? Just walking around the house?"

"I was trying not to think about that."

Mark goes over to the TV/VCR and unplugs it. He lifts it up and we walk out of Alex's room.

"Well, that was easy," he says.

We go out the back door. Mark and I carry the

TV/VCR together. It feels like lead in my arms. This is going to be a long walk home.

"Hey guys," a voice says behind us.

Mark and I look at one another. Fear rises in my throat. Who's after us now?

"What are you doing?" another voice asks.

We turn around.

I breathe a sigh of relief.

It's Nate. He's with his friend Ana. She's an eighth grader at Scarecrow Middle School too. I don't know her very well, but she seems cool.

"What are you doing with that old TV?" Ana asks.

"Uh," I say, unable to think of anything that sounds normal.

"We're fixing it," Mark says quickly. "For Alex. He bought it, but it doesn't work. My dad is handy, so he's going to fix it."

"Oh," Ana says, smiling. "It's so cool. Is it from the '80s?"

I shrug.

"Hey, that reminds me," Ana continues. "Are you guys going to the dance tonight?"

"No," Mark and I say in unison.

"You should! It's '80s-themed. Everyone is dressing up. Doesn't that sound fun?"

"Not really," Mark says.

"I'm going," Ana says. "So is Nate."

"Cool," I say.

"Well," Nate says. "We better bounce. We're going to get a hamburger."

"You want to come?" Ana asks.

"Nah," Mark says. "We need to get this to my dad. It's kind of heavy."

"Later," Nate says.

They walk away. We go in the opposite direction.

"Now what?" Mark says when they are out of earshot. "We got this thing. What should we do with it? I don't know anything about cursed TVs or VCRs. Do you?"

Then a thought hits me.

"Hey, maybe we *should* go to that dance," I say.

"What? Why?"

"Alex is supposed to be there with Grace and Kimberly, remember? There's no way he would miss that. If the creature is still inside him, maybe we can catch it. Then we'll destroy the TV!"

"The beast also might be mad that someone took his TV/VCR," Mark says. "What if he attacks us?"

"We're the only ones who know about the creature

inside Alex. We've got the TV/VCR now. You and I are the only people who can stop it."

Mark sighs. "I hate to say it, but you're right. Man, how did Little Alex cause such big problems?"

CHAPTER 18

LET'S DANCE

The dance is awful. Nothing looks '80s except the lighting. They brought in a bunch of multicolored fluorescent lights. These are set up all around the multipurpose room. Kids dance as the lights shine on them. But most of the music isn't even from the '80s. It's just a bunch of pop stuff. Nobody knows any '80s dance moves either.

What's worse is that hardly anyone is dressed for the theme. Mark and I threw together outfits to try to look like Marty McFly from *Back to the Future*. We borrowed a couple of old jean jackets from Mark's dad. I have a puffy red vest over mine. Mark even found a pair of his dad's old high-tops to wear. Most kids are just wearing their normal clothes though.

"This is boring," Mark says.

"Totally." I adjust my vest.

"Can we put this somewhere?" Mark holds up a big

backpack. The TV/VCR is in it. "I'm tired of lugging it around."

"Sure."

It was easier to carry the TV/VCR in the backpack. The teachers at the dance didn't ask about it either. They probably figured it was part of our '80s looks.

We search for a safe spot to set the backpack down.

"What about under the table?" Mark asks.

There's a table with a punch bowl and cupcakes on it. A long, black tablecloth hangs all the way to the floor.

"Perfect." Mark looks around and discreetly lifts up the tablecloth. He slides the backpack underneath it.

"Well," I say. "I guess now we wait to see who shows up."

Mark and I walk around to kill time. We are standing by the fluorescent lights when Grace and Kimberly walk up to us.

"Have you guys seen Alex?" Grace asks.

She and Kimberly are two of the few who dressed up. Grace wears fluorescent yellow sunglasses. Kimberly wears blue ones. They both made their hair big and frizzy too.

"Uh, no," I say. "Not tonight. Haven't seen him."

Talking to girls always makes me nervous. It doesn't matter what the situation is.

"We're here, though," Mark says, smiling.

They don't smile back. "Let us know if he shows up," Kimberly says. "We've been looking for him all night."

The girls walk away. If we weren't friends with Alex, they probably wouldn't talk to us at all.

"All right," Mark says. "Let's bail. This dance is bumming me out."

"Okay, but then what are we going to do?"

"We destroy the TV. That thing stole our best friend. It's time to get rid of it."

"Not yet," I say. "If we destroy it now, that creature inside Alex might stay there forever. We have to get it out of him and back into the TV/VCR first. Then we can destroy it."

"Fine, whatever," Mark sighs. "Alex isn't here. Let's just go."

"Maybe we should look for him at his house again?"

Mark and I go over to the table where we left the backpack. He lifts up the long tablecloth.

"It's gone!" Mark gasps.

"Did a teacher find it?" I say.

Then we hear laughter. I look in the direction of it. My heart drops.

Rusty and James have set up the TV/VCR near the dance floor. Both of them are staring at the big black dot on the screen.

"Some TV!" Rusty shouts. "All it shows is a black dot. TV in the '80s was lame!" He and James crack up. A few other kids come over to look too.

Suddenly, the slimy creature bursts out of the screen. It roars so loudly, everyone on the dance floor stops to see what's going on.

"Not again!" Rusty screams. James looks like he's about to cry. Both boys turn and run.

The beast watches them with its glowing green eyes. Then it leaps after them onto the dance floor.

People start running in all directions. Everybody is screaming now. In an instant, the fall dance has become a riot!

"It's trying to get them for picking on Alex," Mark shouts.

"Get the TV!" I yell, running toward it.

Mark beats me to it. He picks the TV up and rips the cord out of the wall. The screen goes black.

"Now what?" he asks.

"We have to destroy it!" I say.

"But you said the creature had to be—"

"It's not in Alex! That's what matters!"

Out of nowhere, Grace and Kimberly run up to us.

"Help us!" Grace says, crying.

"There's no way out!" Kimberly says.

At first, I don't know what she's talking about. Then I smell something. Is that smoke? I look behind us. In the panic, people must have knocked over the fluorescent lights. They were too close to the curtains that cover the windows in the multipurpose room. Some of the curtains have caught fire!

I turn back around to see the beast running through the crowd. It leaps in the air. Now it's coming right for us.

"Mark!" I scream.

Then Alex appears. Where did he come from?

He opens his mouth wide. The beast jumps into it.

"Gross!" Grace and Kimberly scream. They try to run away but Alex blocks them.

"You don't know how great it is!" he yells. "It's the best thing that ever happened to me."

The girls look horrified. They turn and try to run the other way. Alex grabs them both.

I step in between them, grabbing Alex's wrists. Grace and Kimberly seize the moment and take off.

Alex's eyes turn bright green. They look just like the beast's. He twists my arms, breaking my grip. Then he picks me up by the shoulders and throws me across the room.

I land on the cupcake table, hitting the back of my head. Pain shoots through my body. Everything hurts. It feels like I can't move.

Smoke fills the room. More curtains are burning now. Someone has pulled the fire alarm. The noise is deafening.

I see Mark near the flames holding up the TV/VCR. He's going to throw it into the fire!

Then Alex turns his bright green eyes toward him.

CHAPTER 19

FADE OUT

You guys never wanted me to be anything," Alex screams. "I was always just Little Alex to you. Well, that's not who I am anymore!"

Alex opens his mouth. It's so wide, it almost looks like his head has split in two.

The creature flies out of his mouth and jumps on Mark.

Time stands still as we watch the TV/VCR soar through the air. A few seconds later, it lands in the punch bowl. Punch splashes all over my face.

I spring to my feet. Everything still hurts, but I can't think about that right now.

Mustering all my strength, I pull the TV/VCR out of the punch bowl. In the process, I knock the bowl over. It shatters on the hard floor. Glass and punch go everywhere.

"No!" Alex screams.

The green-eyed beast roars too. It leaps through the air, coming right at me.

Adrenaline rushes through me. I lift the TV/VCR over my head and hurl it into the air.

The creature is still flying toward me. Its bright green eyes are glowing with rage.

With a crunch, the TV/VCR lands in the fire.

A high-pitched scream like nothing I've ever heard comes out of the creature. It's so loud, I have to cover my ears. Everybody else does too. The cry is more deafening than the fire alarm.

The creature lands a few feet in front of me. It crumples to the ground. Both of its eyes have become black circles. They look exactly like the dot that played on the TV screen.

It's no longer screaming. Actually, the beast looks sad. I feel kind of bad for it.

The creature becomes jittery. It shakes harder and harder. As it does, the color seems to leave its body. For a moment, the beast looks like black and white TV static. Soon it's nearly transparent. I realize it's disappearing.

"Ahhh!" I hear Alex cry. He shakes too, but he isn't disappearing.

A few seconds later, the creature is gone.

I run over to Alex and Mark. Alex is quiet now.

"What happened?" he asks. "Where am I?"

We look around at the melee. Alex seems to have no idea he caused it.

Most people have gotten out, but a few are still running around frantically. Flames continue to spread. Water is raining down from the ceiling sprinklers now. The whole place is thick with smoke.

"We'll tell you later," I say. "We need to get out of here!"

Mark and I grab Alex. We head toward the front entrance. At least we think that's where we're going. It's hard to tell through all the smoke and water.

Breathing is getting harder. We're all coughing a lot. The room is so hot now too. It feels like my puffy red vest is melting.

"I . . . see . . . the exit!" Mark chokes.

We're going to get out!

Suddenly, a silhouette appears in front of us. It's huge and stocky. A creepy tube hangs off its dark face. And it's holding an ax!

"Come on!" the silhouette shouts.

The monster reaches for us. We pull away. Whatever or whoever this is won't get us!

We squint as light floods our faces. The monster

has a huge flashlight. Then I realize it's not a monster at all. It's a firefighter.

A bunch more of them burst in with a long hose. They run past us and start spraying down the flames. Smoke billows out the doors as we are taken to safety.

CHAPTER 20

VINTAGE RETURN

The door of the Vintage Rose Antique Shop jingles when we open it. Mark carries what's left of the TV/VCR. It's half-melted. The entire screen is shattered.

"No refunds on that," the kid behind the counter says. "I don't care what happened. It's not my fault."

A girl in jeans and a black T-shirt walks out from the back. "What's going on, Jay?" she asks.

I recognize her from school. She's an eighth grader. Her name is Tenley, I think.

Mark sets the TV/VCR on the counter.

"I can't believe how heavy that thing still is," he says, shaking his arm.

Tenley looks at it.

"This is *that* thing, isn't it?" she asks. Tenley touches the back of the TV/VCR. "From the fire at the school dance?"

"Yeah," I say. "Were you there?"

"No. I was working. My friends told me about it though."

"Well, I bought it here," Alex says. "We didn't know what to do with it, so we're returning it."

Ever since the beast disappeared, he's been totally normal. He seems to have no recollection of what happened. Alex doesn't remember the creature or the crazy stuff he did. That's probably why he didn't get in trouble. His mom has just been taking him to the doctor for checkups.

"That's fine." Tenley smiles at Alex. "We'll take care of it."

"*You* will!" Jay snaps. "I'm not touching that thing."

"Don't mind my brother," Tenley says. "How much did you pay for this?"

"Uh, ten dollars," Alex says.

"Twig! You can't give him his money back," Jay protests. "The item is destroyed! What will we tell Mom and Dad?"

Tenley shoots her brother a look. "We *have* to," she says. "Or the deal isn't done."

Jay scowls as she opens the cash register and takes out a ten-dollar bill.

"Here you go," she says, handing it to Alex.

"Wow, thanks!" Alex is obviously stoked to have

his cash back. "Sorry about all the trouble I caused."

"Maybe you should lock that thing up so nobody else gets it," Mark suggests. "We heard it might be cursed or something."

"Oh, don't worry," Tenley assures him. "We have a safe place for stuff like this. It won't get out again."

We leave the Vintage Rose. After getting rid of the TV/VCR, it's like a weight has been lifted. I feel so relieved.

"Glad that's over," Mark says as we're walking down the street.

"Me too. Want to get some candy to celebrate?" I ask.

"Yes!" Mark smiles.

"I can't," Alex says, frowning. "Tomorrow is the quiz in Mr. Harlin's class. I'm so behind on my homework."

"Dude," Mark says. "You heard Mr. Harlin is out for at least a month, right? Don't worry about homework!"

"No, I really can't," Alex says. "My mom expects me home. See you guys later." He walks away.

Mark and I continue toward Reggie's.

"Hey, I thought you were going to start trying harder in math," I say.

Mark sighs. "Yeah, I know. Okay, we'll just make a quick stop at Reggie's. Then homework."

"Let's get some candy for Alex too," I suggest. "We can take it to his house and study there."

"Good plan!"

Mark and I have been working on treating Alex better lately. We're not giving him such a hard time. When we're deciding what to do, we include him. Neither of us calls him "Little Alex" anymore either.

At Reggie's, I get a big chocolate bar. Those are my favorite. Mark chooses a bag of sour cherry balls. We buy Alex some chocolate-covered marzipan. He loves that stuff. After paying, we make our way to Alex's house.

When we knock on the door, nobody answers.

"That's weird," Mark says. "Maybe he just isn't expecting us. Let's try the back door."

We walk to the back of the house and peek through Alex's window.

Alex is sitting on his bed. He holds his school tablet close to his face.

From where I'm standing, I can just make out what's on the tablet. My body goes cold inside.

"He digitized it," I say.

"What?" Mark asks, confused.

"He put the video of the black dot on his tablet!"

Alex fixates on the big black dot. Every so often it changes into a black triangle. This must be why he was always holding the tablet so close to his face. Somehow he transferred the video from the tape onto it!

"The creature is going to come back," I say.

Then Alex opens his mouth wide.

"I think it's already happening!" Mark says.

Suddenly, Alex stands up. He looks straight at us through the window. Mark and I freeze in fear.

We start to scream. Then a wide smile spreads across Alex's face. He walks over to the window, laughing at us.

"Alex!" Mark yells. "Come *on*!"

We run through the back door and bust into his room. All three of us are laughing now.

"Bro," I giggle. "That was not cool!"

"Did you really put the video on your tablet?" Mark asks.

"I did. But don't worry. It's deleted now. That was just a fake," Alex says. "After hearing how much trouble that thing caused, no way did I want to bring it back. Besides, my throat still hurts!"

"Phew," I say. "Want some candy?"

Alex takes the chocolate-covered marzipan. "Thanks, Donovan!"

"We figured we could all do homework together," Mark says.

Alex smiles. It's good to have our friend back.